BAGELS THE BRAVE!

Joan Betty Stuchner

illustrations by Dave Whamond

ORCA BOOK PUBLISHERS

To Tom and Dov, as always,
and to Cindy and my friends.

Text copyright © 2015 Joan Betty Stuchner
Illustrations copyright © 2015 Dave Whamond

Library and Archives Canada Cataloguing in Publication

Stuchner, Joan Betty, author
Bagels the brave / Joan Betty Stuchner; illustrator: Dave Whamond.
(Orca echoes)

Issued in print and electronic formats.
ISBN 978-1-4598-0493-7 (pbk.)—ISBN 978-1-4598-0494-4 (pdf).—
ISBN 978-1-4598-0495-1 (epub)

1. Dogs—Juvenile fiction. I. Whamond, Dave, illustrator II. Title.
III. Series: Orca echoes
PS8587.T825B337 2015   jC813'.54   C2014-906689-9
                              C2014-906690-2

First published in the United States, 2015
Library of Congress Control Number: 2014952069

Summary: In this sequel to *Bagels Come Home*, the Bernstein family heads off on a camping trip
to Sasquatch Lake, only to encounter a series of mysterious happenings.

Orca Book Publishers gratefully acknowledges the support for its publishing programs
provided by the following agencies: the Government of Canada through the Canada Book Fund
and the Canada Council for the Arts, and the Province of British Columbia
through the BC Arts Council and the Book Publishing Tax Credit.

RECYCLED
Paper made from
recycled material
FSC® C103567

*Orca Book Publishers is dedicated to preserving the environment and
has printed this book on Forest Stewardship Council® certified paper.*

Cover artwork and interior illustrations by Dave Whamond
Author photo by Tom Kavadias

ORCA BOOK PUBLISHERS   ORCA BOOK PUBLISHERS
PO Box 5626, STN. B   PO Box 468
Victoria, BC Canada   Custer, WA USA
v8R 6s4   98240-0468

www.orcabook.com
Printed and bound in Canada.

18 17 16 15 • 4 3 2 1

CHAPTER ONE
We're Going Camping (Sort of)

I'm Josh Bernstein, and I'm excited.

Why? Because the Bernstein family is going camping for three whole days.

I hope Bagels is coming with us. He's my dog. He's a mutt—a mix of sheltie, Jack Russell and whippet.

He's a great dog—except that he can't keep still and he doesn't do what he's told. But nobody's perfect, right?

We've never been camping before. My sister Becky's almost six. I'm eight. That's pretty old never to have been camping.

"Will there be bears?" I ask.

"Not where we're going," says Dad.

1

"What about lions?" asks Becky.

"Nope," says Mom. "A few squirrels, maybe. Possibly a skunk or two."

It'll be Becky's birthday while we're away.

"I'll bake a cake on the trip," says Mom.

Mom? Baking on a camping trip?

Becky asks if she can bring Blanky. Blanky's a baby blanket she's had forever. It used to be yellow. Now it's closer to gray.

"Sure, bring Blanky," says Mom.

"We can sleep in the tents Aunt Sharon gave us!" I say.

"Actually, it's not that kind of camping," says Dad. "We've rented a cabin. Like the pioneers lived in."

"That's not camping," I say.

"What's a pioneer?" Becky asks.

"They're those long-ago people who didn't have televisions or bathrooms," I explain. "They hunted for food because there were no supermarkets."

Becky says she doesn't want to be a pioneer.

"There'll be a bathroom where we're going," Mom says. "And we'll take food with us. Josh, stop scaring your sister."

"What about TV?" says Becky.

"There isn't one," says Dad.

"Can't we be pioneers in a motel?" Becky asks.

"We don't need TV," says Dad. "We'll play board games and talk to each other. It'll be fun. Now, where did I put Snakes and Ladders?"

Talk? Board games? No TV? How is that fun?

"Can Bagels come?" I ask.

Dad gives me a look that says, "Does he have to?"

As I said, Bagels isn't perfect. But Becky and I love him. Besides, he's a talented stage actor. I know acting isn't much use on a camping trip. But a couple of months ago, Bagels appeared in the Marpole Players' production of *Peter Pan*.

Okay, he wasn't *supposed* to be in *Peter Pan*. Mom and Dad were the lead actors. Bagels was supposed to be at home. But he's an escape artist.

Becky and I think that on *Peter Pan* night, our cat Creamcheese opened a window for him. She likes to get him into trouble.

Bagels arrived at the theater and ended up onstage.

It was my fault, so I'm lucky the audience loved him. In fact, the director wants him in next year's production of *Pup in Boots.*

Since then, we've had our windows fixed. Now they're dog- *and* cat-proof.

There's just one thing. Becky and I haven't told Mom and Dad that Bagels can also open doors.

CHAPTER TWO
Camping Plans

"Of course Bagels is coming," says Mom. "He's a great guard dog." She means he barks anytime someone comes to the door. He barks extra loud for the mail carrier.

He also eats the mail. And the mail carrier's learned not to put her hand through the mail slot anymore.

Becky and I have worked really hard to get Bagels to behave. He hasn't jumped in the neighbor's fish pond for a long time. It helps that our neighbor put chicken wire over the pond after Bagels frightened his fish to death.

Bagels still rounds up joggers. That's because he thinks they're sheep. We're working on that and on the mail-eating problem.

It's not his fault he's a slow learner.

Dad frowns at Bagels. Bagels grins back at him.

"Bagels can't get into much trouble camping," I say.

We all know that's not true.

"Fine," says Dad. "But this is his last chance. If he doesn't behave on this trip, he can go live on a farm. Lots of space. Lots of sheep."

Becky and I look at each other. We're not going to let that happen.

"Where's the cabin?" I ask.

"Sasquatch Lake," says Dad.

"Who'll take care of Creamcheese and Lox?" I ask. Lox is our goldfish.

Mom says Aunt Sharon's taking care of the house while we're away.

We're not leaving until next week. Becky drags out her little pink suitcase anyway and starts packing.

Oh well, I might as well start packing too. I drag out my brown case *and* my Dad's big old army duffel bag.

7

The first things I pack are my alligator flashlight and my camera.

I also find a couple of other things that might come in handy.

More on that later.

CHAPTER THREE
Sasquatch Lake, Here We Come

Aunt Sharon stands at the door and waves to us. She's holding Creamcheese. Creamcheese is squirming, but Aunt Sharon is pretty strong.

"Have fun being pioneers."

Creamcheese sneers at Bagels. I can read her mind. She wants him to get into trouble at the lake. She hopes he won't come back.

As we fill the trunk, Dad eyes the duffel bag. "Josh, we'll only be gone three days. Why so much luggage?"

"Always be prepared," I say.

"Wow," says Dad. "And you're not even a Boy Scout."

9

You ain't nothin' but a hound dog, a-cryin' all the time...

Dad's playing an Elvis CD. Dad and Bagels both love rock 'n' roll. It's the one thing they have in common. Mom doesn't like Elvis. She says his grammar is poor. Bagels is perched between Becky and me in the backseat. He sings along with the King.

... you ain't never caught a rabbit...

"Rooroo, wah, wah, wah..."

...and you ain't no friend of mine...

Dad drives and sings. Mom holds the map.

"Turn right here," says Mom.

Dad turns right.

"Left at the next light," says Mom. Dad obeys.

They do this until we finally reach the lake.

It's in the middle of a hilly forest. I see a few farms close by.

There's a signpost. *Sasquatch Lake: Pioneer cabins ahead.*

Something moves behind the signpost.

I see a hairy face.

I blink.

It's gone.

Weird.

We park near a shack. It looks haunted, like something from a horror movie. *The Shack at Haunted Lake.* There's a sign on the door. It says *Forest Glade.* That sounds like the name of an air freshener.

"Honey," says Dad, "are you sure this is it?"

11

Mom takes a brochure from her purse. It says *Sasquatch Lake Map*.

She opens it up.

"This is it."

She takes a key out of her purse.

I look at the shack. Are those holes in the roof?

"I saw a motel back on the highway," says Becky. "I bet it has TV."

I forget to put Bagels on the leash *before* we get out of the car. There are ducks on the lake. He sees them. He grins and does a backflip. Then he runs to the lake and dives in.

He swims in circles. The ducks cuss at him in duck language.

Mom opens the trunk of the car. She and Dad take out the luggage and the groceries. Becky grabs her pink suitcase.

Dad looks at Bagels and shakes his head.

"One more chance," he says to me.

Then he takes the groceries into Forest Glade.

"Bagels," I yell, "get out of the lake right now."

Bagels thinks I've said, "Stay in the lake, Bagels, and annoy the ducks."

He keeps it up for a few more minutes. Then he barks, dips his head in the water and comes up with a fish in his mouth.

He swims to shore, scrambles up the bank and runs in circles around me. Then he runs past me. Then he dances a jig.

I take a photo. Bagels drops the fish. It flips. It flops. It lies very still.

Bagels does a shimmy shake. Water flies everywhere.

"Here, Bagels," I say, patting my leg.

He grins. He chases his tail. Then he skids to a stop. He looks at the forest. He stiffens. His hair stands on end.

A twig snaps. A bush trembles.

A deer, maybe? A squirrel? Or a skunk!

What if there *are* bears?

I grab Bagels's collar just in time. He growls. I pick him up. I pick up the dead fish.

"Bagels," I say, "you are *not* going to get into any more trouble."

He struggles. I hold on tight.

The fish doesn't struggle.

I think it's kind of dead.

CHAPTER FOUR
Forest Glade

"Bagels caught dinner?" says Dad.

Mom wants to know what kind of fish it is.

"It has fins and scales," Dad says, "and it's fresh. That's good enough for me."

I look around the cabin. It doesn't *smell* like a forest glade. It smells funky. Also, I was right. There *are* holes in the roof.

Lucky for us, the forecast says sunshine for the next three days.

"Josh, you and Becky will share a room," says Mom.

"Bunk beds!" Becky shrieks from our room.

She wants the top bunk. Fine with me.

While Becky unpacks, I head for the kitchen.

15

Mom and Dad are there. So is Bagels. He's racing around the kitchen.

Dad's brewing coffee. "Josh," he says, "please feed Bagels."

I find a can of Meaty Delight and put some in Bagels's bowl. Bagels stops racing and starts eating. By the time I've helped Mom put away the groceries, Bagels has licked the bowl all around the kitchen.

"When you've unpacked, you kids can take Bagels for a walk in the forest," says Mom. "Only don't go too far."

She looks around the kitchen. Then she opens the window. "What we need in here," she says, "is some fresh air."

I'm not sure Mom's ready to be a pioneer. Dad hands her a coffee.

"Don't forget to take your mom's cell phone," he says.

I go to my room and unpack my suitcase.

I leave the duffel bag in a corner.

"Be prepared," I say to myself. I grab Mom's cell phone.

CHAPTER FIVE
A Walk in the Forest

"Why is Bagels on his leash?" asks Becky.

Bagels wonders the same thing. It's a long leash, but he still pulls on it.

I don't tell Becky about the hairy-faced guy. I don't tell her about the snapping twig or the shaking branches. She's only five. Well, six tomorrow.

Bagels sniffs the ground in all directions.

"Bagels," I say, "what's wrong?"

He doesn't answer.

"This forest is dark," says Becky. "Can we go back now?"

"Soon," I say.

Part of me wants to know what Bagels has sniffed out.

Part of me doesn't.

"What if we get lost?" says Becky. "Like Hansel and Gretel?"

I pat my pocket. "We have Mom's cell phone. They didn't."

Bagels whimpers. "Hmmm. Hmmm."

He's scared. Bagels is *never* scared.

If *he's* scared, there's something scary out there.

"Okay, Becky," I say. "I'm with you. Let's go back to Stinky Vines."

"Forest Glade," says Becky.

"Right."

"Bagels," I say, "let's go." Bagels doesn't move. He just whimpers.

"Josh, why is Bagels making that scaredy-noise?"

I tell her I don't know. It's like Bagels has been hypnotized.

Dad must have been wrong. It has to be a bear.

"Keep very still," I tell Becky. I try to remember the rule about bears. Do you make a lot of noise or no noise? I know that climbing a tree is out.

I hear rustling.

Becky whispers, "Whazat?"

"I don't know. Shh."

Bagels turns. He looks at me—terrified. Then he flies into my arms.

I fall backward. On Becky.

"Owww."

"Sorry, Becky."

I look over Bagels's shoulder. I expect to see a grizzly bear.

But I don't see a bear. I see two sheep. Actually, one of them is a lamb.

Becky squirms out from under us. She sees the sheep.

"Awww!" she coos. "A lamb! Look, Josh, a baby lamb and its mommy."

"Well," I say, "it's sure not a grizzly bear."

I stand up with Bagels still wrapped around my neck. He's choking me.

"Josh, what's wrong with Bagels?"

"I'm not positive," I say, "but I think he's afraid of the sheep."

"But he's part sheltie," says Becky. "He rounds up joggers."

"Well, Becky, I guess he's not afraid of joggers."

The lamb and its mom skip away, bleating happily.

"Behe, behe, behe."

Bagels clings tighter.

"Bagels," I croak, "they've gone. You can get down now."

He looks over his shoulder. He waits. He jumps down. This time I wrap the leash twice around my wrist.

We head back to the cabin. Poor Bagels keeps looking over his shoulder. Becky and I agree not to tell anyone about Bagels being afraid of sheep.* It might not be too good for his image as a guard dog.

---

*Anyone who has a fear of sheep suffers from *ovinaphobia.*

CHAPTER SIX
Pioneer Dinner

When we get back to Forest Glade, it doesn't smell funky anymore. It smells of grilled fish.

Our first meal at Sasquatch Lake is delicious.

Bagels mostly plays with his food.

"Bagels has lost his appetite," says Dad. "That's not like him."

Becky and I stay quiet.

Dad's cell phone starts to play "All Shook Up." Bagels perks up a little. It's one of his favorite Elvis tunes.

Dad answers the phone. "Bernstein summer residence," he says. Then he frowns.

"Who is this?"

There's a pause.

"Someone's breathing heavily," says Dad. "Now he's grunting."

"May I see?" I ask. He hands me the phone. I check the screen. Mom's number is on it.

"Oh no," I say. I check my pocket. No phone. "I must have lost Mom's phone. Someone found it."

I put the phone to my ear. "Hello. Did you find our phone? Who is this, please?"

I hear sounds like the ones Dad makes when he falls asleep in front of the television at home. Or like the big gorilla in that movie *King Kong*.

The phone goes dead.

I must have dropped the phone when Bagels leaped on me.

"What did he say?" asks Mom.

"Nothing," I say. "He just breathed funny and grunted."

"Maybe he'll phone back," says Dad.

Before bedtime, we have a glass of milk in the kitchen while Mom reads to us from *Peter Pan.* Becky and I both like that story. It reminds us of Bagels's first acting gig.

My favorite line is *Second star to the right, and straight on till morning.*

When we go to bed, Mom closes the door to the kitchen.

"So Bagels won't escape through the open kitchen window," she says.

CHAPTER SEVEN
Never Trust the Weather Forecast

Becky hits the top bunk. I snuggle into the bottom bunk. Mom shuts the door. She thinks it will keep Bagels out.

I'm tired. My eyelids are getting heavy. As I start to close my eyes, I see a hairy face at the window. It grins at me. It has big yellow teeth. They look like blank mahjong tiles.

Wow, I'm so tired my imagination's playing tricks on me.

"Weroo, weroo."

I dream there's a dog howling in my ear.

The dream dog stands on my chest. I can't breathe.

I open my eyes. It's not a dream. It's Bagels.

Bagels and Becky have joined me in the bottom bunk.

"What are you guys doing?" I say. I reach under my pillow and take out my alligator flashlight. Becky and Bagels are staring at me. They look scary.

"It's raining on our bed," whispers Becky.

"That's impossible," I say. "The weather forecast said clear skies."

"My bed's wet," she says.

I reach up and touch the top bunk. It's wet.

"Becky," I say, "are you sure you didn't…"

"I'm sure," she growls. She hands me Blanky. It's wet too.

"Maybe Bagels?" I suggest.

"Grrr," says Bagels.

"No," says Becky. "It's rain."

Then I hear it. The rain is coming down pretty hard.

I also hear Mom and Dad in the living room. The light's on in there.

Becky, Bagels and I head for the door. I step in a puddle.

In the living room, Mom and Dad are standing under a picnic umbrella. Mom's wearing a long nightshirt that says *Books are a Girl's Best Friend* on the front. Dad's wearing his Spider-Man pajamas.

Mom says, "Looks like the weatherman lied."

27

Dad smiles a fake smile. "This is just what the old pioneers had to endure. Is this fun, kids, or what?"

"Yip, yip, grr-ip!" Bagels chases raindrops.

"What shall we do?" says Mom.

I'm just about to say something when Bagels rushes to the front door. He growls.

"Rrrrr, grrr, gwrr."

"What now?" says Dad.

Bagels backs away from the door. He does a backflip, then runs back at the door and starts to scratch on it.

"Grr, rrr, weroo, roo!"

We all huddle under Mom's umbrella.

"Listen," she says. We listen.

"What?" says Dad.

"Didn't you hear it?"

We all shake our heads.

"Hear what?" I ask.

Mom frowns. "I heard something out there. Footsteps. Heavy breathing. When Bagels barked, I thought it ran away."

"A bear?" Becky asks.

"This isn't bear country," says Dad.

"Why don't you check, Dad?" says Becky.

"I'm not checking." He looks at Mom. "Why don't you check?"

"I'm not checking," says Mom.

Becky and I look at each other. No chance.

Bagels rushes from the front door to the kitchen door. He barks. He does more backflips.

Becky says, "Bagels wants to protect us. Brave Bagels."

Becky's forgotten about the sheep.

Finally, Dad agrees to check outside. He puts on his baseball cap. He takes the picnic umbrella.

I grab Bagels as Dad opens the front door. He squirms. Bagels, not Dad. Dad steps outside. He opens the umbrella. The wind blows it inside out, and Dad falls into a big mud puddle outside the door.

He gets up, then falls down a second time.

The third time he says, "There's no one out here. May I come in now?" He doesn't sound happy. Mom says he can come in.

Dad has a hot shower. "At least something's working," says Mom.

I've put Bagels down on the floor. He goes back to running and backflipping from door to door. We leave him to it. Becky and I sit under the picnic umbrella, playing Snakes and Ladders. We're starting to think this is kind of an adventure.

Dad comes back wearing a tracksuit.

"How are we going to sleep when the roof's leaking?" he asks.

"I almost forgot," I say. I rush to my room. I head for the big duffel bag.

A minute later I'm back in the living room with two tents.

Becky shrieks. "We're going camping after all."

Dad shakes his head. "Those tents won't stand up to that wind."

"We can pitch the tents in here, Dad."

I press a button on each tent. They pop open like giant umbrellas.

"The kid is a genius," says Dad. I blush. Mom brings in spare blankets and pillows.

Dad and I are in one tent. Mom and Becky are in the other tent. Bagels stops running around. The imaginary bear must have gone.

I fall asleep as soon as my head hits the pillow.

CHAPTER EIGHT
Mystery Burglar

Next morning, I'm awake early. Bagels and Dad are both snoring next to me.

I poke my head out of the tent.

The sun is shining again.

At breakfast, Mom admits the tent wasn't so bad.

Bagels is licking his kibble dish around the kitchen again.

"By the way," says Mom. "Which one of you played a trick on me?"

"What trick?" asks Dad.

"Someone took the peanut-butter jar. And the jar of Great-Aunt Minnie's homemade kosher pickles.

They were right next to the sink. Now come on—own up."

Everyone stares at Mom. I didn't take them. Becky didn't take them.

"Sorry, don't like peanut butter," says Dad.

"Hmm," says Mom. "That's odd."

Mom takes the wet bedding outside, along with Blanky, the Spider-Man pajamas and the baseball cap. She hangs them on tree branches out back.

"What'll we do today?" asks Dad. "Might as well take advantage of the sunshine. There's a rowboat and life jackets behind the cabin."

Sounds like a plan. Only first we have to mop the wet floors.

We've just finished when Dad's phone starts to play "All Shook Up."

He answers.

"Hello, Bernstein summer residence." He listens, then says to us, "It's the grunting guy again."

He looks at the screen. "It's your mom's number, Josh." He hands me the phone.

"Ask him to please return my phone," says Mom.

Bagels looks at the phone. He frowns. He growls. The phone goes dead.

Mom comes back and announces that she's going to bake Becky's birthday cake. "Before anything else goes missing."

"So why don't the rest of us go into the forest and see if we can find your mom's phone?" says Dad.

"Don't run into any trouble," says Mom.

She looks at Bagels. "Take care of the family." Bagels chases his tail, then grins at Mom. "I'll take that as a yes," Mom says.

I put Bagels on the leash in case we run into any scary lambs.

Becky and I try to retrace our steps. Dad follows.

We must take a wrong turn. The forest is thicker here.

Becky stops and points. "What's that?"

Carved into the hillside is a doorway without a door.

"It's a cave," says Dad.

Bagels growls. He's angry. He wiggles his bum as if he's ready to attack. That's a cat move he must have learned from Creamcheese.

We head for the cave.

"Hello," I say at the entrance. No answer. Bagels sniffs the ground. He growls. He smells something, but it's not sheep. He's angry, not scared.

The cave is dark inside. I switch on my alligator flashlight.

"Well," says Dad, "will you look at that."

It's an empty peanut-butter jar. There's also an unopened jar of pickles. I pick it up. It's labeled *Great-Aunt Minnie's Homemade Kosher Pickles.*

"Those are our pickles!" Becky says.

"I see that," I say. The lids on Great-Aunt Minnie's pickle jars are always too tight. Mom usually has to

run hot water on them before she can open them.
Even Dad's not strong enough. That's because Great-Aunt Minnie can bench-press two hundred pounds.

Bagels is still growling. He pulls on the leash.

I pick up the pickle jar. I look around. This cave is a mess.

There are slices of old salami on the ground. They don't smell so good. There's also a scattering of hot-dog wrappers and empty bread bags.

"I think we've found our food thief," says Dad. "Let's go back to Leaky Laurels."

"Forest Glade," Becky and I say together.

"Right," says Dad.

Bagels is the only one who doesn't want to leave. He's looking at the back of the cave and growling. Something's there, I just know it. But what?

All the way back to the cabin, I have the feeling someone is watching us. Bagels feels it too. He's walking backward. Something is very strange.

And I still don't have Mom's cell phone.

CHAPTER NINE
Happy Birthday, Becky (Almost)

The cabin smells of baking.

Dad hands Mom the pickles.

"We found them in a cave," I tell her. "The peanut butter was there too. But someone ate it."

"While you were gone," says Mom, "I bumped into a couple from another cabin. They told me there's been a lot of food stolen lately. Even some clothes. Maybe there's a homeless person living in that cave. If so, we should help him out."

Dad agrees. "Poor guy, having to steal food."

"Meanwhile," says Mom, "take a look at Becky's birthday cake."

We head for the kitchen.

The cake is on the table.

"Whoa," says Becky when she sees it.

It's chocolate on the outside and Mom says it has vanilla icing and custard on the inside. On top is Becky's name in pink icing and a candle shaped like a number six.

I get out my camera and take a photo. It's lucky I do.

"Let's leave it here so the icing sets," Mom says. "How about we go boating now and then eat the cake later?"

Dad looks at Bagels. "You'd better stay here," he says. "There aren't enough life jackets."

"He can wear mine," says Becky.

"Absolutely not," says Mom.

Dad closes the kitchen door so Bagels won't get in.

We're halfway across the lake when Becky asks, "Dad, why do they call it Sasquatch Lake?"

"Just some silly story," says Dad. "One of the old pioneers thought he saw a Sasquatch here years ago."

"What's a Sasquatch?" I ask.

"It's supposed to be some creature that looks like a human but has hair all over its body," says Mom. "Some guy even took a photo of one once. But it was fake."

"How did they know it was fake?" I ask.

"Because," says Dad, "the man who faked it eventually owned up to what he'd done."

"So there's no such thing as a Sasquatch?" asks Becky.

"I doubt it," says Dad.

I wonder.

Just then we hear "All Shook Up." Dad's phone is beside him on the seat. He's busy rowing, so I answer it.

Mom's number shows up on the screen.

"Hello," I say. I hear a grunt.

I also hear Bagels barking in the background.

Then the phone goes dead.

"Dad," I say, "we have to get back."

"Was it the guy who sounds like King Kong?" asks Dad.

I nod. "And Bagels."

Dad rows us back to shore.

As we get out of the boat, I hear Bagels.

"Woof, grr, woof, gerrerr, smrfflllrr."

Dad pulls the boat onto the shore. "What's with Bagels?" he says as they all take off their life jackets and throw them in the boat. All except me. I don't want to waste any time.

I run to the kitchen side of the cabin.

I see someone heading for the forest.

He's wearing Dad's Spider-Man pajamas, a baseball cap and a Hudson's Bay blanket.

"Hey," I shout. The guy turns. His face is hairy. And I mean *hairy*. Only there's white stuff all over it. And something that looks a lot like custard.

He smiles. He has teeth like yellow mahjong tiles. He waves Becky's Blanky at me before he disappears into the forest.

"Dad," I yell as I run into the cabin.

Dad's in the kitchen.

"BAGELS!" he shouts.

"Smrffllr?"

Bagels is sitting on the kitchen table. His mouth is filled with cake.

Becky lets out a wail of woe. "MY CAKE!"

CHAPTER TEN
Bagels Saves Dad

"Bad dog," says Dad.

"It's not Bagels," I say.

"You can't fool me," says Dad. "I'd know that dog anywhere."

"I mean Bagels isn't guilty," I say. "Someone got here before Bagels and ate most of the cake. Bagels is eating the leftovers."

Dad looks at me. "The kitchen door was closed."

Becky breaks the news. "Bagels can open doors, Dad."

"Bagels," I say. I point to the open window. "Go get him."

Bagels cocks his head to one side. He looks at the window. He looks back at the cake leftovers. I can tell he's torn.

He makes the right choice.

He leaps out of the window and heads for the forest. We all follow. Except *we* use the front door.

"Wait for me," shouts Becky. Dad picks her up and puts her on his shoulders. As they run ahead of me, I hear Becky saying, "Giddyup, Dad."

Running uphill is not as easy as you might think. Especially in a forest. Unless you're a sheltie/Jack Russell/whippet.

Bagels barks to let us know where he is. We soon reach him. He's outside the cave—growling. I put him on the leash.

Becky's bedding is all over the place. Mom gathers it up.

"Blanky's not there," says Becky. Dad sets her on the ground.

"Grrrr," says Bagels.

"Josh," says Dad, "before we go into this cave, I need to get something straight. Do you really think that someone climbed into our kitchen and ate most of Becky's birthday cake? The same guy who has Mom's cell phone?"

I nod.

"The homeless guy?" adds Mom.

I nod again. "Except he's not homeless. I think he lives in the cave."

"A cave is not a home," says Mom.

"Maybe not to us," says Dad.

And I think, That's because we're humans, Dad. But I don't say it.

Bagels is pulling on the leash. It's now or never.

As we head into the cave, Dad says, "Josh, let's be careful."

"It's okay," I say. "We have Bagels."

Dad starts to say something. Then he changes his mind. Everyone follows Bagels and me into the cave.

It's empty.

Except for the smelly mess of leftovers.

Mom looks around. "It looks as if the mystery man isn't here," she says. Then she sniffs. "This cave stinks. I'm going back to the cabin. Who's with me?"

Dad and Becky are.

But Bagels smells something else. With his nose to the ground, he pulls on the leash.

"I'll be there soon, Dad," I call as Bagels pulls harder.

Bagels finds a smaller passage at the back of the cave. We zigzag down it.

We go deeper into the hillside. It's darker here. I switch on my alligator flashlight.

Wait...I see an opening. What do you know! The cave has two entrances. Bagels runs faster. He's practically dragging me.

We reach the second entrance. There's only one problem. I realize too late that this entrance has a ten-foot drop...

...right into the lake.

Lucky for me, I'm still wearing my life jacket— and Bagels is a good swimmer.

"Josh! Bagels!" I hear my mother yelling from the shore.

Bagels and I start to swim. Dad's getting in the rowboat to rescue us.

"Werooo," says Bagels.

Dad's rowing like crazy. He reaches Bagels first, leans over and tries to grab him. He leans too far.

Dad falls into the lake.

"Hi, Dad."

"Hi, Josh. Glubblub."

"Weroof?"

That's when Bagels and I learn…Dad can't swim.

Dad's going down for the third time when Bagels bites into his jacket and heads for the shore. They're both doing the dog paddle. Bagels is better at it.

CHAPTER ELEVEN
Another Cake

Mom pulls Dad onto the grass. Bagels jumps on his chest. Dad spits up a lot of water. I didn't know Bagels knew CPR.

"Bagels rescued Dad!" says Becky.

Dad spits up more water.

He opens his eyes. Bagels licks his face.

Dad says a word I've never heard before.

From the look Mom gives him, I guess it's a bad word.

We all help pull Dad back on his feet.

Mom and Dad head to the cabin with Bagels. Becky and I stay where we are.

I look back. I see the cave entrance—or should I say exit? There's someone moving up there. It looks like...Hairy Guy?

Becky sees him too. She squints. Hairy Guy ducks behind a tree. But not before I take his photo.

"Who is that?" asks Becky.

I tell her what I think. Her eyes grow big. "Should we tell Mom and Dad?" she asks.

"Maybe not yet," I say. "But did you notice what he was holding?"

Becky nods. "Blanky," she says. Then she looks me in the eye. "I'm six now. I don't need Blanky anymore. I think I'm ready for a G.I. Joe and a Barbie—and maybe I'll *finally* get that pony."

We go back into the cabin. I hope the water didn't damage my camera.

While Dad, Bagels and I get dry, Mom bakes another cake. She says it's bad enough that poor Becky loses Blanky. She shouldn't miss out on her birthday cake.

Becky says, "It's okay, Mom. Now that I'm six, I don't need Blanky anymore."

Wait till Mom hears what Becky *does* want.

Becky whispers, "I think the hairy guy needs Blanky more than I do."

Sure, I think, but does he need Mom's phone?

Mom's second cake looks good. We all sing, "Happy birthday, dear Becky." Bagels joins in.

Just as we finish the last piece of cake, there's a bright flash.

And it's not my camera.

It's lightning. Followed by a drum roll. That's thunder. A second later, rain starts to pound on the roof. Two seconds later it pours *through* the roof.

Dad looks up and says, "You know what I think we should do?"

We all nod. "Go back home."

CHAPTER TWELVE
Bagels the Brave

Don't be cruel to a heart that's true...

"Woo, woo, woo, woo-ooooo bruff..."

It's still raining as we drive away from the cabin.

I check my camera to see if it got waterlogged. Luckily, it didn't.

I flip through the pictures until I find the last one. The one I took after we got out of the lake. I press the zoom. Yep. There's the cave entrance. And right beside it is Hairy Guy wearing a baseball cap and Dad's pj's.

As we turn onto the highway, I see something in the bushes. It's *him*. He's waving Blanky.

I look at Becky over Bagels's head. She sees him too. She grins.

Elvis isn't singing anymore. Neither are Bagels and Dad.

Bagels curls up on the seat.

He's soon snoring.

Dad says, "You know, kids, I've been thinking. Bagels may not be perfect, but he has three things going for him. He's a good actor. He loves Elvis. And he saved my life. Maybe we should forget the sheep farm. All those who agree, say aye."

Becky, Mom and I say, "Aye."

"Motion carried," says Dad.

Bagels doesn't know what a lucky escape he's had.

I try not to think how disappointed Creamcheese is going to be.

Bagels twitches in his sleep.

I think he's having a good dream. Maybe he's rounding up joggers.

"Dad," I ask, "is it okay for Bagels to sleep with me tonight?"

"Sure," says Dad. "Just this once."

"Okay," says Mom, pointing at the map. "Second turn to the right and straight on till we get home."

CHAPTER THIRTEEN
The End (I Hope)

I wake up in my own bed. Bagels is sharing my pillow. He's snoring. But that's not what wakes me. I hear music. Elvis is singing "All Shook Up." Oh no. I forgot to give Dad his phone back. Should I answer it? I look at the alarm clock. Two AM? Who's phoning Dad at two in the morning?

Wait a minute. I think I know who.

"Grrrr," Bagels growls at the phone. He knows too.

Only a Sasquatch would be phoning this early in the morning.

I switch off the phone. I lie back down.

"I can't remember if Mom's phone has GPS," I say to Bagels.

Bagels doesn't answer.

He's snoring again.

I fall asleep trying to figure out how long it would take for a Sasquatch to walk all the way from Sasquatch Lake to our house.

Too long.

I hope.

Joan Betty Stuchner loved stories. When she wasn't writing, she worked in a library, taught part-time and acted in community theater. Sadly, Joan lost her battle with cancer in 2014, but her stories will continue to bring joy to readers for years to come.